HOCKEY_SLAND

ISBN: 978-0-578-61026-9 (hardcover)
ISBN: 978-0-578-97275-6 (paperback)

3Sisters Publishing
Cape Cod, Massachusetts

DEDICATION

This book is dedicated to our parents, Dorothy Margaret DeMirjian Kishibay and Charles Ohannes Kishibay for their unique ways of storytelling. Mother with her paintbrush and flare for the creative interpretations while Dad used his music, words and numbers. As children we were introduced to the art of storytelling from Broadway to the back porch where music and tales sailed across the floor capturing all attendees on life's natural highs and lows.

Special thanks to my husband, James W. Hobbs for his love, support, patience and believing.

Welcome to Hockey Island. You are about to experience an Island that is way north off the coast of Greenland, not far from the northern tip of Kaffeklubben Island.

Many live on the Island from children, to adults, dogs, cats, hamsters, seals, ducks, seagulls of course, and the occasional goose.

Do you want to live on Hockey Island? Well if you do you must bring your Imagination...

3

...Imagine that every day
there is a full moon...

...Imagine that it snows all day long each and every day...

...Imagine that there are no paved streets or roads, but ice filled alley ways that meander across the Island that many scoot about, bypassing frozen ponds, waving at neighbors and fellow skaters, enjoying the glow of shimmering roof tops and jack frost playing on the windows...

9

...Imagine one lighthouse that spooks the Island with its strobing light and romances skilled captains and sailors alike...

11

...Imagine that everyone who lives on Hockey Island skates really well...Imagine that there are hockey teams that wager games every day of the week... Imagine it and it is so.

13

Now legend has it, that the Island Shaman, a spiritual leader and teacher, spoke of the Snow Moon that shines over the Island each and every night. In true glory it rises like a giant peach in the sky, radiating bright orange as it climbs to its magical spot way above the lighthouse lantern room...

...The legend went on to say that if you stared at the full moon long enough you can see it tap dancing among the stars, creating whimsical notes of music carried across the Island and beyond. Melodies from Brahms, Tchaikovsky, Mozart, Bach, Common and Kygo.

Midnight skating is quite the norm on Hockey Island especially when the moonbow appears. It takes a special evening with the hint of a breeze gently brushing the faces of the skaters who have come out to draw their figure 8's on the ice. The clouds playfully move into attention, protecting the moon, creating a prism of colors across the night sky.

19

One of the brightest businessmen on the Island, Maxwell Connor, lives his life by 3 simple things: Dream. Believe. Achieve. He noted the Islanders needed something warm to drink as they spent all their days skating from place to place, house to house and pond to pond.

One night he dreamt of a giant hot cocoa machine. The next morning he believed he could do it.

And that same day he achieved it by buying a brand new, shiny cement mixer. It was a truck, the only vehicle on the whole Island.

Soon before the eyes of the children he filled the mixer with gallons of milk, pounds of cocoa powder, a few thousand marshmallows, a pinch of cinnamon and many tablespoons of ingenuity.

The day finally arrived. Max flipped the switch on the mighty truck. The engine began a slow roar. Soon the mixer started to jiggle, the milk and cocoa mixed together creating a gurgling noise like a morning belly waiting for a bowl of hot oatmeal.

The slow churn got faster and faster and soon Max's Mocha Machine was going round and round like a Ferris wheel at a town fair.

Minutes later down the chute, came a frothy, bubbling mixture, sweet to the taste and oh so creamy. The Islanders filled their heart shaped mugs and knew they had something very special to enjoy.

21

23

Living on the Island is the famous, 'Lollipop Cowboy' or George as his family calls him. A strong young boy that has been playing hockey since he was five. He can always be found skating through the Island, rallying up a hockey game or two, proudly wearing his cowboy hat and tasting the blue raspberry twists of his giant lollipop.

25

Near the edge of the harbor is a sweet seaside bungalow that is George's home. Tucked amid large sand dunes that are most often frozen, George feels safe and cozy in his cabin by the sea even when the winds whip up the coast.

27

His boat, Wave Walker II, moored right next to his home in the harbor, plays dodge ball with the waves most of the time. Many days and nights, the wind whistles across the inlet, parading waves into the shore, bowing and thrusting their might spraying their salty slap on those that dare to stand close to the shore's edge which many times George has done.

Often when out on his boat, George finds incredible treasures that he safely tucks into his 'sailor's valentine' a lucky eight-sided box, an antique souvenir given to him by his Popi as he returned from Barbados, an island in the West Indies.

George has protected all that is important to him in his 'sailor's valentine'; from the hockey puck that he swung into the winning goal seconds before the game was over, to sea glass, clam shells and even tarnished, ocean worn coins from a pirate ship that sank many years ago off the coast.

31

On his bedroom wall is a treasured gift, a ship captain's light from Pirate Bill, an old time sea captain that often ate too much rum cake and told George he found the light in the depths of the ocean.

George loves how the light shines brightly about the room and plays peek – a- boo with the nighttime darkness, comforting those that pass by with its warm glow.

33

The houses are tight and small, but long into the night the windows glow with warmth shining brightly on the snow covered lawns, casting giant shadows from the trees that embrace the edges of this seaside hamlet.

The warm glow joins the bending moonlight combined with the strobe from the lighthouse creating shadow characters on the snow. This makes nighttime into fun time.

35

Just past the harbor, where George lives, is the home of a young girl, Ella Sophia, the only figure skater on the whole Island. She makes magic as she skates in and out of the moonbow colors cast along the ice.

Her flippy skirt made of seaweed and feathers graces her legs as she moves angling her skates, following her reflection on the ice. Her favorite color is pink and she loves anything that glistens, like snow, crystals and glitter.

Smiling, as she gracefully arcs her arms and hands performing her style of skating Tai Chi. Her peaceful flow calms her soul and breaking on her face is a blissful smile.

Some would say she's flirting with the boys that line the edge of the pond, but Ella knows her smile comes from within, her inner bliss, her safe spot of sheer happiness.

In the deep of the winter the multicolored Northern Lights, or aurora borealis, dance across the arctic sky. Hockey Island has the best view in the whole region so when they appear, skaters from far and wide come to dance their magic on the ice, playing hide and seek among the colors waving at them from afar.

The most experienced skaters, led by Ella Sophia, line up like the New York Radio City Rockettes and with precision and form they kick high and spin low, leading the Islanders in synchronized skating, filled with the spirit of the night.

39

Right around the New Year, when the Northern Lights are their brightest, a gentle breeze speaks across the Island – 'Wind Words' the Islanders call it, which means 'words from the heart.'

Love for One Another
Peace to the World
Freedom for All
Spirit in Our Hearts
Kindness to Everyone
Simplicity to Live By

Love

Peace

Freedom

Spirit

Kindness

Simplicity 41

THE END

Manifesting inside your hearts is your,
Magic, Imagination, and Creativity.

Color the World in Love ™

Dora Verne Kishibay Garabedian, Our mentor and big sister who taught us how to view life in wonderment and surprise by marveling at every sunrise and sunset and insisted we eat our hot dogs with relish and mustard with an occasional splash of sauerkraut. She taught us the art of exploration while watching for shooting stars in the back yard on an August night, to the world of story telling and had us mesmerized by little boys circling the moon in their very own spaceship. A fashion goddess and essential oil guru, we thank her for our first pair of hip hugger jeans, strumming her guitar, and filling her room with burning incense.

Karen Yvonne Kishibay, Always looking for her horse, she is the savant of the family, her creative, restless mind always pushing the limits of what a conservative household would allow. That innate curiosity led her to illustrate this book. Her magic to bring to life any form or situation is God given and through her years she has led us down many creative paths. Passing by chances to be a dancer and actress, she transformed the written word into characters designed to entice any teacher's curiosity. Her creative eye does not miss much. Wanting to live as an artist in a loft in New York City she still gives thanks to the angels for quick drying white paint!

Darby Marya Kishibay Hobbs, Born under the astrological sign of Sagittarius, half horse, half man, she is Karen's lost horse. A child at heart she learned to 'make believe' at a very young age, from being a teacher to imaginary students and grading their very real papers, to dressing up wearing Mom's jewelry strewn around her neck and force fitting her shoes into Mom's high heels. She never stopped pretending. This innocence led her to foresee tall tales and whip words into magic, which fills the pages of this book. Wanting to be a New York Radio City Rockette, she is a storyteller and teacher at heart – a Shaman – her purpose is to move the reader on an exploration of their soul.